Jules Verne (1828-1905)
was born in Nantes, France.

Around the World in 80 Days
was first published in 1873.

This edition published by
Coles, Canada
by arrangement with Brompton Books Corp

© 1993 Brompton Books Corp

Produced by
BROMPTON BOOKS CORP
15 Sherwood Place,
Greenwich, CT 06830,
USA

Directed by CND – Muriel Nathan-Deiller
Illustrated by Van Gool-Lefèvre-Loiseaux
Text adapted by Sue Jackson

ISBN 1 85469 911 3

Printed in Hong Kong

VAN GOOL'S

Around the World
in 80 Days

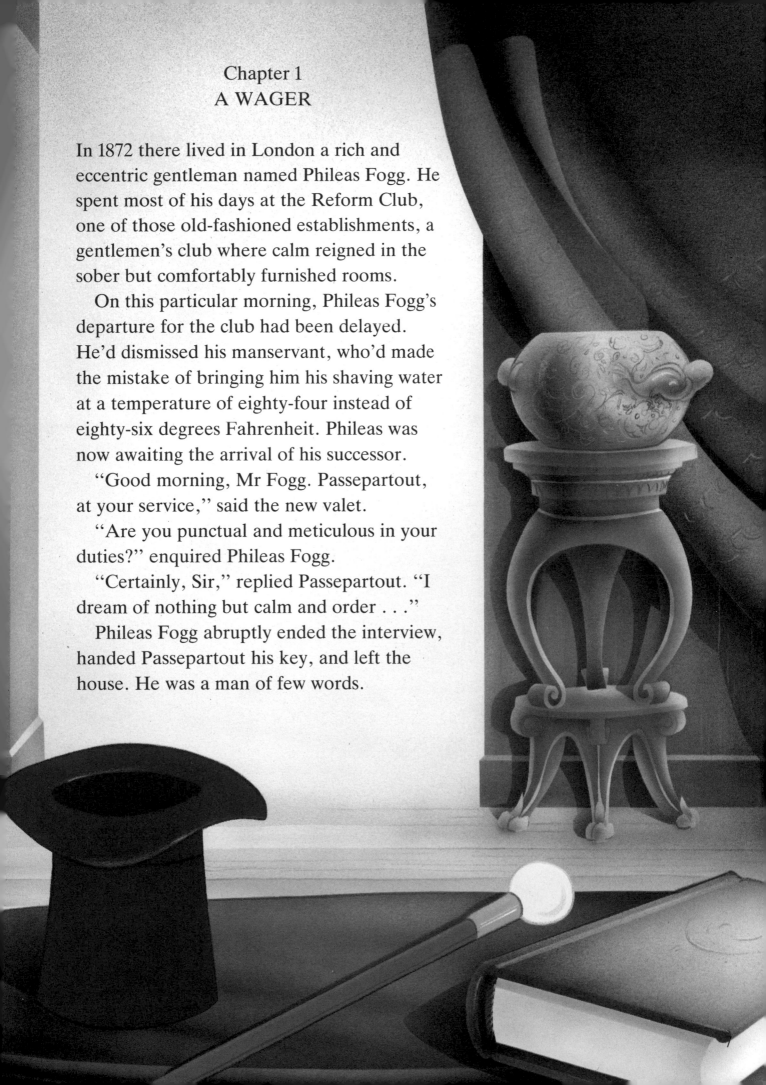

Chapter 1
A WAGER

In 1872 there lived in London a rich and eccentric gentleman named Phileas Fogg. He spent most of his days at the Reform Club, one of those old-fashioned establishments, a gentlemen's club where calm reigned in the sober but comfortably furnished rooms.

On this particular morning, Phileas Fogg's departure for the club had been delayed. He'd dismissed his manservant, who'd made the mistake of bringing him his shaving water at a temperature of eighty-four instead of eighty-six degrees Fahrenheit. Phileas was now awaiting the arrival of his successor.

"Good morning, Mr Fogg. Passepartout, at your service," said the new valet.

"Are you punctual and meticulous in your duties?" enquired Phileas Fogg.

"Certainly, Sir," replied Passepartout. "I dream of nothing but calm and order . . ."

Phileas Fogg abruptly ended the interview, handed Passepartout his key, and left the house. He was a man of few words.

Every afternoon, Phileas Fogg played cards. On this afternoon, the conversation was unusually animated: the Bank of England had just been robbed of £50,000.

"The police have a good description of the culprit. Inspector Fix is on the case, and officers have been sent to all the ports in Europe and America," reported one of the club members.

"They will never find him once he has left the country. The world is so vast, he could disappear almost anywhere," stated another.

"The world's not as large as you think, gentlemen," interrupted Phileas Fogg calmly. "I would wager that I could make a tour of the world in eighty days."

"But could *you*?" asked one of his acquaintances. "You hate travelling, my friend, and enjoy nothing more than your routine, ordered existence."

Phileas Fogg slowly rose to his feet. "I will prove that it's possible! Today is 2 October. I will be back in London, at the club, on Saturday, 21 December, at a quarter to nine precisely. I wager £20,000 that I will succeed. If I miss the appointment, the money is yours!"

Phileas Fogg returned home immediately and informed Passepartout that they were leaving for a tour around the world.

"But, Sir . . . " stuttered Passepartout, dazed.

"Pack only a carpet bag with two shirts and three pairs of stockings for each of us," continued Phileas Fogg. "We'll buy what we need on the way. Make haste, we don't have a moment to lose."

"But Sir, I was advised that you were a phlegmatic gentleman not disposed to rash or impetuous actions. I've just resigned from the service of a reckless young gentleman, and I was looking forward to some peace and . . ." Passepartout could see that his words fell on deaf ears.

Ten minutes later the bag was packed. Phileas Fogg, the Continental Railway and Steam Guide tucked under his arm and a large roll of Bank of England notes in his pocket, left the house with his new valet to catch the quarter-to-nine train to Dover.

Chapter 2
THE INSPECTOR OF POLICE

Inspector Fix arrived in Suez. He was convinced that Phileas Fogg was the man who had robbed the Bank of England. Fogg answered the description of the thief, and had left the country on the day of the crime. It was just too much of a coincidence! Inspector Fix had, therefore, followed Phileas Fogg and his manservant across Europe, and was now lying in wait to arrest them. His only problem was that he had no jurisdiction in Suez. He decided to pay the British Consul a visit.

"The infamous Bank of England robber is here in Suez. His name is Phileas Fogg. Would you kindly detain him until the warrant for his arrest arrives from England?" he asked.

"I'm afraid that's not possible, Inspector," answered the Consul. "Mr Fogg's papers are entirely in order and I can't withhold his passport. That would be illegal!"

Fix was indignant. What could he do?

It was vital that the inspector did not lose sight of his quarry. He boldly approached Passepartout in the street.

"Excuse me," he said politely, "I can see that you are a visitor here. Do you plan to stay long?"

"No, Sir," replied Passepartout. "I had dreams of a quiet existence in London, but my master has dragged me off on a madcap venture. We are to tour the world. Our next port of call will be Bombay."

Fix considered his dilemma. "Well, if the warrant doesn't arrive in time," he thought, "I shall just have to proceed to India."

After a calm and uneventful sea crossing, our three intrepid travellers landed in Bombay without having lost any precious time. To record their arrival, Phileas Fogg went to have his passport stamped.

Passepartout, on his way to the railway station (closely followed by Inspector Fix), spied a beautiful temple. He could not resist the temptation to step in. But no sooner had he put a foot over the doorstep than he was attacked and his shoes were dragged off his feet. Poor Passepartout! How was he to know that he had to remove his shoes before entering the temple? Totally confused and barefoot, he ran to the station and boarded the Calcutta train. Once he had recovered his breath, he went in search of Phileas Fogg, who was already installed in his compartment.

"Passepartout, you might have missed the train," said Phileas Fogg sternly. "And look at the state you're in!" Passepartout tried to explain, but the train was off.

17

The train made an unscheduled stop.

"End of the line. Please leave the train," cried the guard.

No one had thought to warn our travellers that the railway line, which was supposed to cross India, had not been completed! It would take several years before the two sections of track, one from the east, the other from the west, met. Like the other passengers, they would have to make alternative arrangements to rejoin the line. Phileas Fogg's solution was to continue the journey by elephant! There wasn't a second to spare if they were to catch the boat from Calcutta.

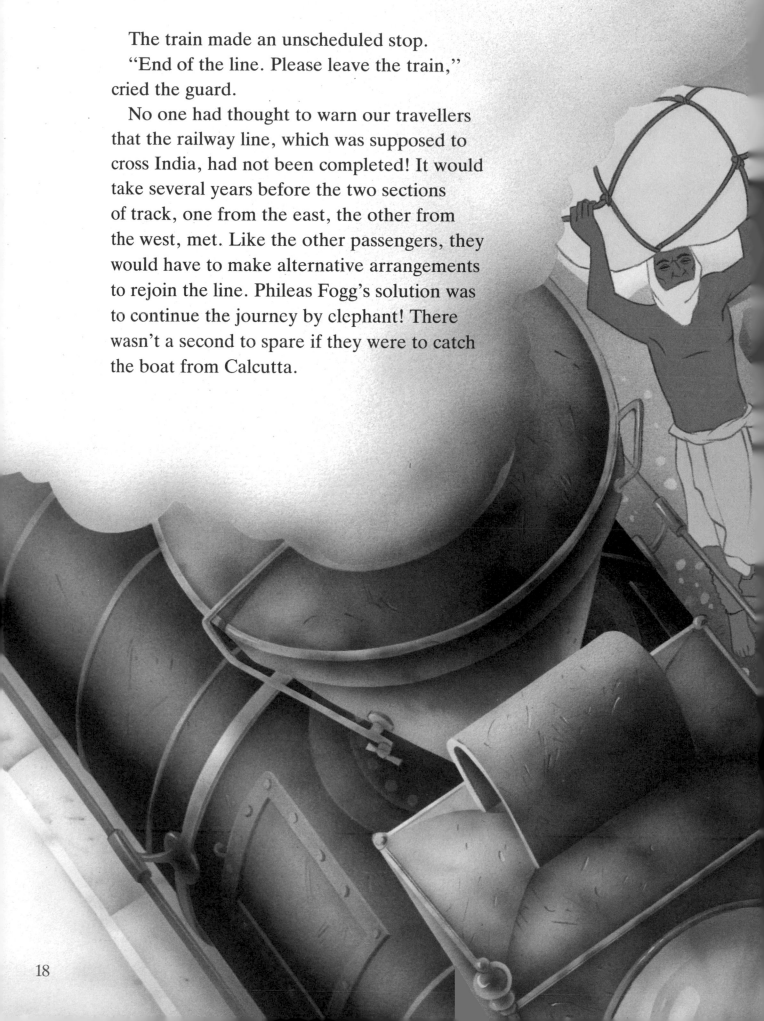

Chapter 3
THE COURAGEOUS VALET

Perched in a howdah on the elephant's back, Passepartout could hear chanting in the distance. He turned to the mahout for an explanation.

"It is a religious procession," replied the guide. "If you want a closer look we must approach discreetly. Can you see a beautiful young woman in the middle of the crowd? She is the rajah's wife, the rani. The rajah has died, and it is the custom here for a wife to burn with her husband's corpse. Tomorrow Aouda must mount his funeral pyre."

"We can't abandon this woman to her fate," declared Phileas Fogg. "We'll act tonight."

"But Sir, you don't have a choice, and anyway we must consider the wager!" reminded Passepartout.

Yet again Phileas Fogg was not listening.

Passepartout thought his master was mad. How were they going to get anywhere near the woman? She was surrounded by priests and the guards of the rajah's retinue. But like his employer, Passepartout was not one to admit defeat easily.

Long after midnight, Phileas Fogg and Passepartout circled the temple where the rajah's wife was imprisoned. It was securely guarded and entry impossible.

In the morning, the young woman – heavily drugged – was escorted to the pyre. She was lifted up and placed next to the body of her husband. Phileas Fogg was about to launch himself forward and snatch her from the executioners, when he heard the crowd cry out, "Look! Look! The rajah lives! He has his wife in his arms! It's a miracle!"

The multitude prostrated themselves on the ground, and Passepartout – for it was him, in disguise – hurried down from the pyre. The young woman had fainted in his arms.

"Quick, let's leave!" he panted.

They mounted the elephant and fled. The rani had been rescued, but at what cost! Valuable time had been lost!

"Where am I?" murmured Aouda, when she awoke several hours later.

"You have been saved from the pyre, Madam," announced Phileas Fogg. It had seemed like a nightmare but gradually she remembered everything – her detestable husband, the barbaric custom of suttee . . .

"Oh! Sir," she said, turning to Phileas. "I shall be forever in your debt. If you had not rescued me, I would now be a pile of ashes." Totally overwrought, Aouda threw herself at his feet.

"Stand up, Madam," said Phileas Fogg stiffly. "It was just a matter of Passepartout being quick witted, nothing more."

"What is to become of me now?" she cried. "I can no longer remain in India."

Phileas Fogg enquired whether she had any relatives abroad. On learning that her cousin had settled in Hong Kong, he declared, "That's settled. You must accompany us. Hong Kong is our next port of call."

"If we're lucky enough to catch the boat," murmured Passepartout.

Our voyagers boarded the *Rangoon* in Calcutta minutes before it set sail. They were hardly out at sea when Passepartout bumped into Inspector Fix.

"We meet again! You must be following us!" said Passepartout jokingly.

Inspector Fix was a tenacious man. The warrant still hadn't arrived but, knowing Phileas Fogg's destination, Fix had pursued him across India. "My dear Sir, what a pleasure to find you here!" he said, feigning surprise. "Are you also travelling to Hong Kong?"

"As you see," replied Passepartout. "And a young lady, who has just been snatched from the jaws of death, has joined our party." He proceeded to tell Fix about the adventure.

Passepartout decided that Fix had been engaged by the Reform Club to spy on them. However, once he spotted Hong Kong, all thoughts of Inspector Fix vanished from Passepartout's mind.

"My goodness, Hong Kong is teeming with people," sighed Passepartout, greatly impressed with the hustle and bustle of the island. Phileas Fogg remained detached and disinterested. Very little made an impression on him.

Unfortunately, Aouda's cousin had long since left Hong Kong, but Phileas Fogg didn't flinch. "Well Madam, we'll have to continue the voyage together," he said.

"But Sir, you're too generous. I could never repay your kindness," she replied.

"We'll say no more," decided Phileas Fogg. Passepartout was sent to reserve berths on the liner *Carnatic*, leaving for America late that evening.

Fix, who was lurking in the background as usual, overheard their conversation. Tired of running after the cursed Phileas Fogg, he decided to adopt a new strategy.

"Passepartout," he called, "come for a drink. You can book the tickets later."

Several drinks later, Passepartout was unable to carry out his master's command. He was slumped over the tables, snoring loudly. He had been tricked!

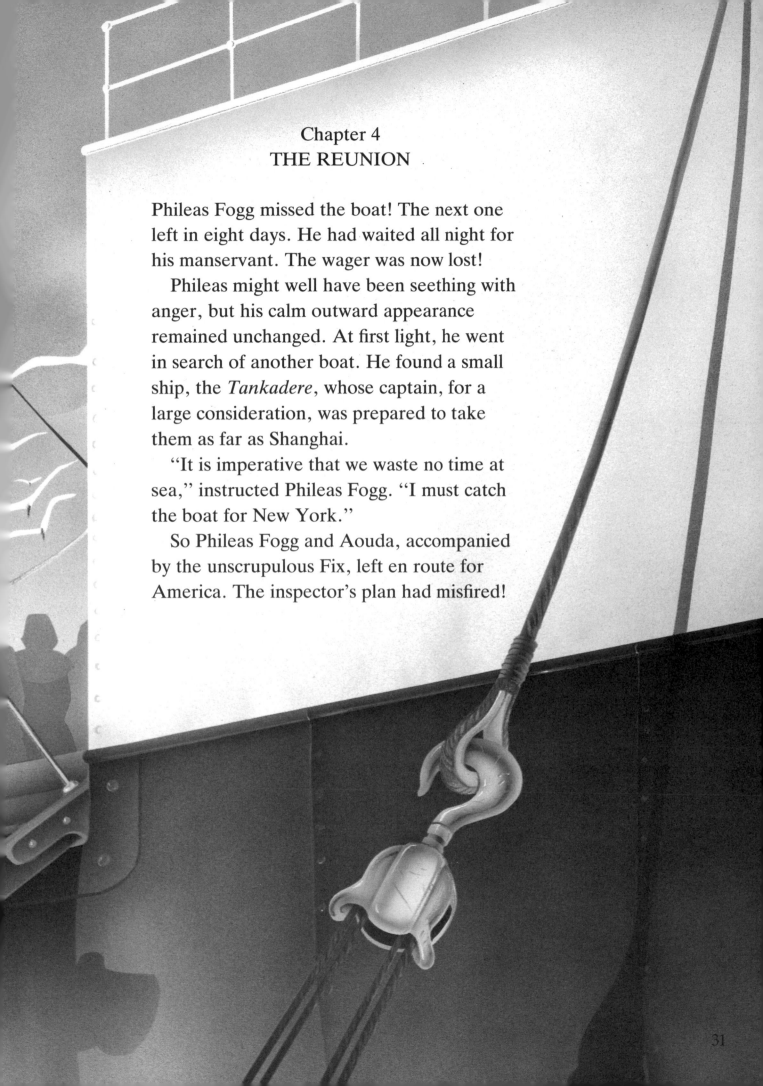

Chapter 4
THE REUNION

Phileas Fogg missed the boat! The next one left in eight days. He had waited all night for his manservant. The wager was now lost!

Phileas might well have been seething with anger, but his calm outward appearance remained unchanged. At first light, he went in search of another boat. He found a small ship, the *Tankadere*, whose captain, for a large consideration, was prepared to take them as far as Shanghai.

"It is imperative that we waste no time at sea," instructed Phileas Fogg. "I must catch the boat for New York."

So Phileas Fogg and Aouda, accompanied by the unscrupulous Fix, left en route for America. The inspector's plan had misfired!

While the other three were sailing away, what had become of Passepartout, abandoned in Hong Kong?

When he awoke, several hours after Fix had left him, Passepartout was miserable. Not only did he have a thumping headache but he was mortified – he had failed in his duty to his master. Gradually the events of that afternoon came back to him. A strong impulse directed his steps to the harbour. He staggered onto the *Carnatic* before he passed out, once again.

The following morning, in the hope that Phileas Fogg had also boarded the liner, Passepartout searched for his employer but he soon discovered that he was stranded without his protector. When he disembarked at Yokohama, Japan, several days later, he was penniless.

How was he going to eat? How was he going to return home? Passepartout considered his situation and decided that there was only one solution: he'd have to find work.

"There, what an interesting poster," noted the valet. "*Last performance of the Grand International Circus before its departure for America*. This is just what I need. A strong and agile man like myself should have no problem gaining employment."

The director of the circus was impressed by Passepartout's biceps and his acrobatic talents. He was engaged on the spot. That evening, while performing as the anchor man for a human pyramid, Passepartout spied his master in the crowd. He rushed forward. The clowns tumbled to the ground.

It was indeed Phileas Fogg. The *Tankadere* had been intercepted by the Yokohama steamer, and Phileas Fogg and his small party had arranged passage to Japan without stopping in Shanghai. Phileas Fogg had learnt of Passepartout's arrival from the shipping company, and had therefore spent all day searching for his faithful, if errant, servant.

"Aouda has decided to accompany us to England," reported Phileas Fogg factually. "Thank goodness we're reunited and can now proceed to join the steamer, the *General Grant*, which leaves soon for San Francisco."

Chapter 5
PACT WITH THE DEVIL

No sooner were our voyagers aboard than Passepartout ran into Fix. He lunged at the inspector. "Tell me, what's your game? I'm sorely tempted to break every bone in your body."

"Listen to me," quaked Fix. "I'll explain, and you'll find we're in agreement."

"Really?" exclaimed Passepartout. "You never cease to amaze me!"

Fix, at last, confided his suspicions to Passepartout. "So you see, we both want the same thing. You want your master to arrive in London, as quickly as possible, to win his wager. And I want him to return speedily so that I can arrest him for the robbery. Why should we quarrel?" Fix was relieved when Passepartout's grip loosened. He was no longer in danger of being thrown overboard.

The valet was puzzled. How could his master, a gentleman, be a common thief? However, if he could establish a truce with Fix, the voyage could be completed without further incident. Passepartout's face broke into a smile. "Alright, let's shake hands. We'll talk about this again," he said.

In San Francisco, our four friends – who had now become inseparable (Fix had been introduced to Phileas Fogg and Aouda during the voyage) – took a walk through the city before catching the train for New York.

Aouda was deep in thought. The more time she spent with Phileas Fogg, the more her feelings for him grew. Her gratitude had turned to affection and now . . . she was falling in love with him.

Phileas remained calm and dignified. He was courtcous but cold, polite but distant.

At last it was time to board the train for New York. The journey was comfortable but unremarkable until, high up in the mountains, the train suddenly stopped.

42

"What's the matter?" Phileas Fogg asked the driver, who had been talking excitedly with the signalman from the next station.

"There is a bridge, further along, which spans the river. It is in a poor state of repair. We don't think it will support the weight of the train," he replied.

"Do you mean that we are stuck here?" asked Passepartout.

"It would appear so, unless . . ."

"Unless what?" queried Phileas Fogg.

"We could attempt a crossing, but it is very risky. If I stoke up the engine and launch the train across at great speed, the bridge might not collapse until we are on the other side. It is possible, but dangerous."

"Go! And there will be a bonus for you, if you succeed," was all Phileas Fogg said.

The engine was stoked, the wheels started to race. The passengers held their breath. Was this the end? No! The train sped across. Behind them, there was a mighty crash as the bridge tumbled into the abyss!

Chapter 6
SIOUX ATTACK

The journey continued across the Great Plains of America. New York was still far away when, above the steady rhythm of the train, the passengers heard blood-curdling war cries and the sound of galloping horses. The train was being attacked by Indians! A number of Sioux had boarded the train, and gained control of the engine.

"There's an army fort several miles ahead," cried the conductor. "If we pass that we're in enemy territory, and shall all be scalped!"

Where was Passepartout? He was no longer amongst the passengers. The brave valet had slipped out of the car, and with amazing agility was running along the top of the carriages towards the engine cab. Unseen, he uncoupled the safety chains. The engine forged on, while the carriages gradually slowed down and came to a gentle stop not far from the fort.

"The soldiers from the fort will protect us now," announced Phileas Fogg.

The passengers breathed a sigh of relief. But where was Passepartout? He had not returned. He had been taken prisoner by the Indians!

"We must raise the alarm at the fort, and set out immediately," declared Phileas.

"But what about the wager?" asked Aouda, moved by the great man's determination. Phileas Fogg did not reply. His only concern, at that moment, was Passepartout's safety.

Aouda and the determined Inspector Fix had a long wait ahead of them. Phileas Fogg left the fort with a detachment of soldiers. Within a few hours, another engine had been coupled to the train and it left . . . without our heroes.

There was no way the wager could be won now. Time was running out. But, more importantly, would Aouda and Fix ever see Phileas Fogg and Passepartout alive again?

In the early morning, Aouda heard horses returning to the fort. There had been a fierce battle with the Sioux Indians, but her heroes were safe!

"Sir! You saved my life, but now you will be ruined. I have never had such a master," Passepartout babbled with gratitude.

"That's enough!" said Phileas Fogg sternly. "Let's consider the matter. We haven't sufficient time to wait for the next train. What alternative transport can we find to cross this windswept plain?"

That was it! The wind! An American, who was accustomed to shuttling between forts on his land sledge, approached and offered to take them to the next city. The sledge was equipped with sails and, despite the discomfort of travelling in the open air, our travellers were soon installed on a fast train to New York.

Once in New York, however, they discovered that the boat for England had set sail – three-quarters of an hour before their arrival! They were stranded in America until the next crossing in a week's time. The wager was lost and Phileas Fogg ruined!

"Come, my friends, we'll book into a hotel and consider our options in the morning," said Phileas Fogg stoically.

He showed no emotion. Although Aouda was worried about the future, she knew that Phileas Fogg would resolve matters. His phlegmatic and disciplined approach would win the day. Passepartout was also learning to appreciate his master's detachment. "You would think he was cold and disinterested," he confided to Inspector Fix. "But really no opportunity escapes him. He's so resourceful. What an amazing gentleman!"

While Passepartout and Fix were discussing his virtues, Phileas Fogg had succeeded in negotiating four berths on a cargo ship leaving for France. The captain was not in the least eager to have passengers aboard his vessel, but Phileas Fogg knew how to handle the man, and a large sum of money exchanged hands.

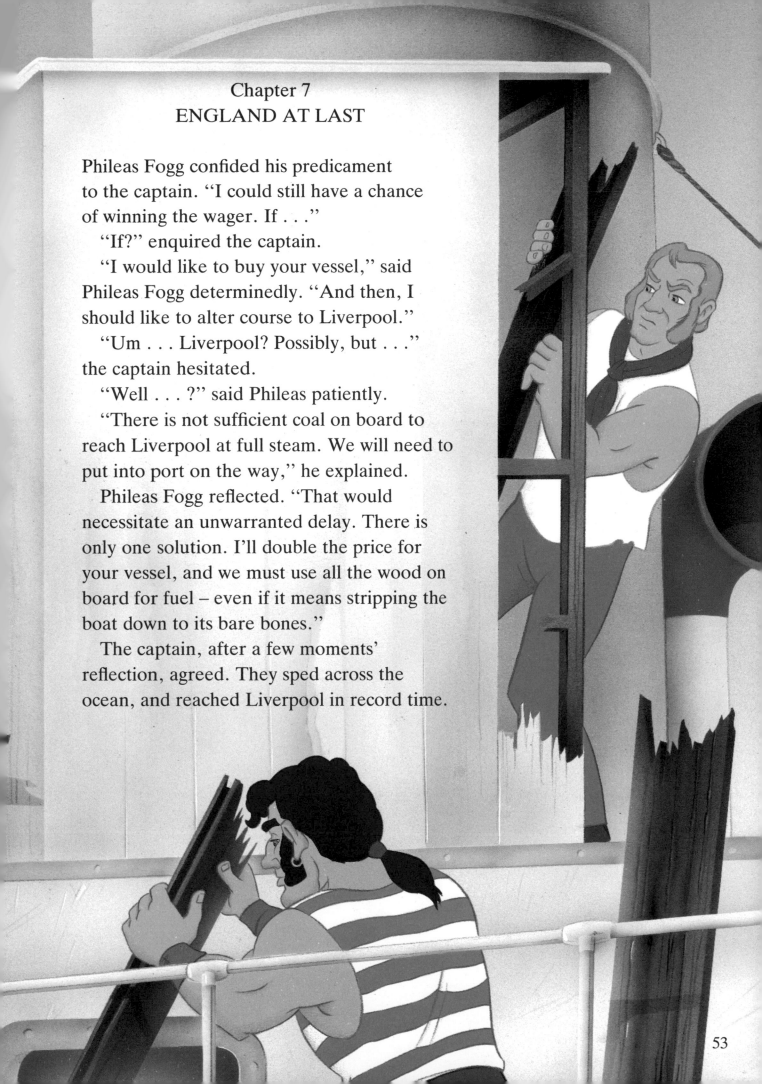

Chapter 7
ENGLAND AT LAST

Phileas Fogg confided his predicament to the captain. "I could still have a chance of winning the wager. If . . ."

"If?" enquired the captain.

"I would like to buy your vessel," said Phileas Fogg determinedly. "And then, I should like to alter course to Liverpool."

"Um . . . Liverpool? Possibly, but . . ." the captain hesitated.

"Well . . . ?" said Phileas patiently.

"There is not sufficient coal on board to reach Liverpool at full steam. We will need to put into port on the way," he explained.

Phileas Fogg reflected. "That would necessitate an unwarranted delay. There is only one solution. I'll double the price for your vessel, and we must use all the wood on board for fuel – even if it means stripping the boat down to its bare bones."

The captain, after a few moments' reflection, agreed. They sped across the ocean, and reached Liverpool in record time.

The moment he set foot on English soil Phileas Fogg was arrested by Inspector Fix and thrown into prison.

"Sir," announced Fix triumphantly, to the Commissioner of Police. "I have caught the most renowned thief of our time. This gentleman is responsible for the Bank of England robbery. In the line of duty, I have followed him around the world."

"What are you talking about?" demanded the Commissioner. "The guilty man has been behind bars for some weeks now. Phileas Fogg is innocent!" Fix rushed to free him, proffering profuse apologies, but Phileas Fogg didn't have time to listen. He caught the next train for London accompanied, of course, by Aouda and Passepartout.

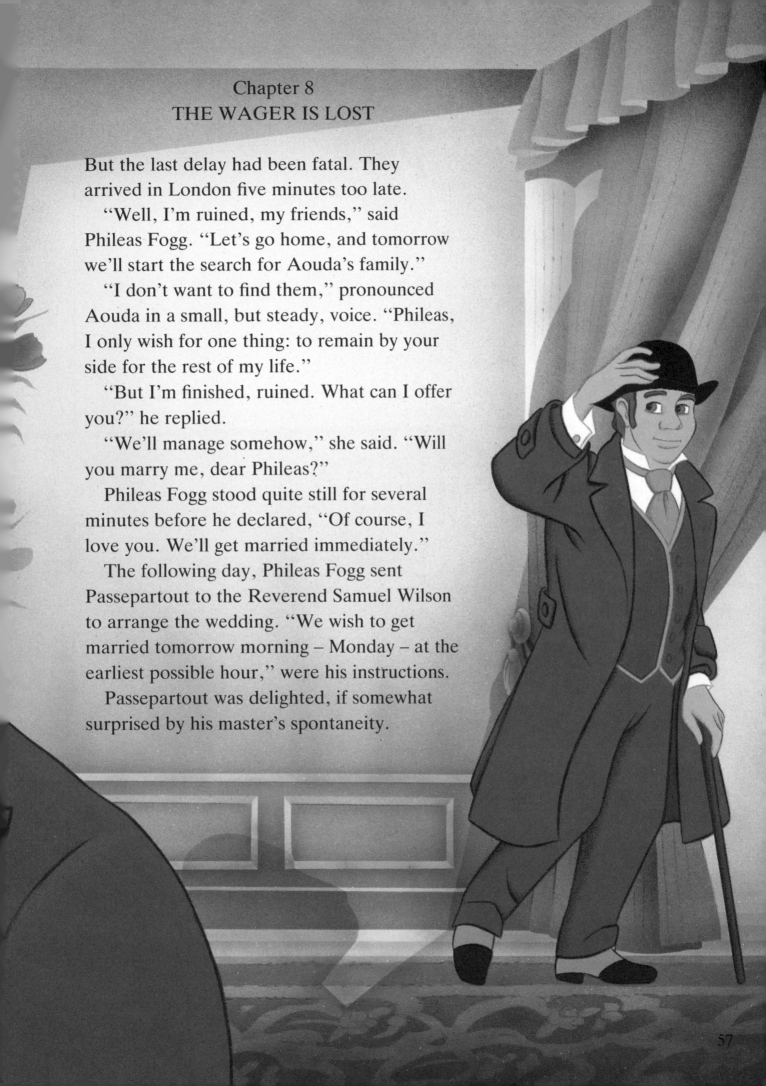

Chapter 8
THE WAGER IS LOST

But the last delay had been fatal. They arrived in London five minutes too late.

"Well, I'm ruined, my friends," said Phileas Fogg. "Let's go home, and tomorrow we'll start the search for Aouda's family."

"I don't want to find them," pronounced Aouda in a small, but steady, voice. "Phileas, I only wish for one thing: to remain by your side for the rest of my life."

"But I'm finished, ruined. What can I offer you?" he replied.

"We'll manage somehow," she said. "Will you marry me, dear Phileas?"

Phileas Fogg stood quite still for several minutes before he declared, "Of course, I love you. We'll get married immediately."

The following day, Phileas Fogg sent Passepartout to the Reverend Samuel Wilson to arrange the wedding. "We wish to get married tomorrow morning – Monday – at the earliest possible hour," were his instructions.

Passepartout was delighted, if somewhat surprised by his master's spontaneity.

It was Saturday evening at the Reform Club and the time was twenty minutes to nine.

"He's lost his bet. He left England eighty days ago and we've had no news. Poor Fogg is ruined and, on his return, he will be the subject of much ridicule."

"Don't cry victory, yet! We still have several minutes before the appointed hour," interjected another club member.

"He must be stranded in America, or Japan. How we will miss him at the Reform Club," conjectured yet another.

Sixteen minutes to nine. There was a commotion in the entrance hall.

"Good evening, gentlemen!" said Phileas Fogg calmly. He had won the wager!

What a surprise! Phileas Fogg, the king of accuracy, had overlooked one detail. Despite his meticulous calculations, and in his chase against time, he had forgotten that if you tour the world from east to west you gain twenty-four hours. So he had arrived in London, not on Saturday, but on Friday evening. This fact Passepartout had discovered on arrival at the clergyman's house, and had rushed home to tell his employer.

So Phileas Fogg had won the wager. Financially, his gain was small; the expenses for the voyage amounted to almost £19,000. What remained he gave to his loyal servant.

But our hero had gained a prize worth more than a fortune – a charming woman who made him the happiest of men!

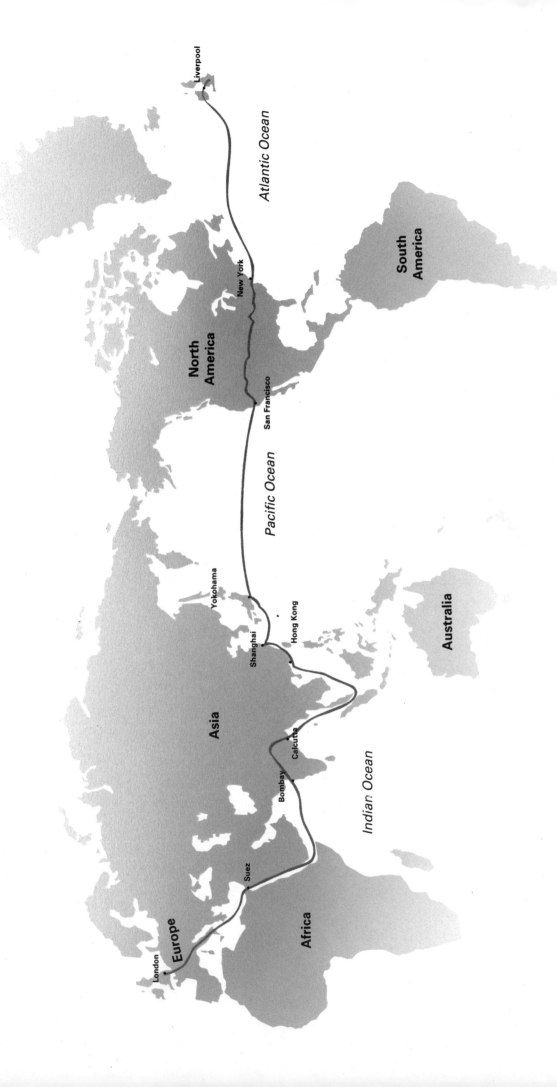